I had written her story and drawn her again and again,
but this little girl I knew so well still did not have a name.
Then I came across the Inuit name **Immi** *and knew it was right for her.*
It was only much later that I found out **Immi** *is short for* **Immiayuk***,*
meaning **echo***, a word that seems very fitting for this story.*

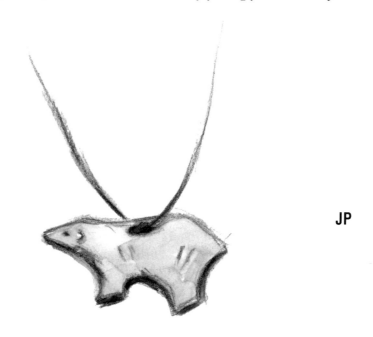

JP

A promise kept . . . Jim and Cilly Littlewood
K. L.

First published in Great Britain in 2010 by Gullane Children's Book
This paperback edition published in 2011 by
Gullane Children's Books
185 Fleet Street, London, EC4A 2HS
www.gullanebooks.com

1   3   5   7   9   10   8   6   4   2

Text and illustrations © Karin Littlewood 2010

The right of Karin Littlewood to be identified as the author and illustrator of this work has been
asserted by her in accordance with the Copyright, Designs and Patents Act, 1988.
A CIP record for this title is available from the British Library.

ISBN: 978-1-86233-823-4

Printed and bound in China

IMMI

by Karin Littlewood

GULLANE
CHILDREN'S BOOKS

Oh, it was cold.
The icy wind blew, and the snow fell and fell.
Immi looked around her, but all she could see
was a frozen, white world.

Immi broke a hole through the ice and fished for her supper.
"Just one more," she thought, "in case anyone comes round..."
which they hardly ever did.

But, instead of a fish, at the end of the line
she found a little wooden bird.

It was so beautiful!
She'd never seen
such colours before.

And she tied it to her necklace,
next to a small white bear.

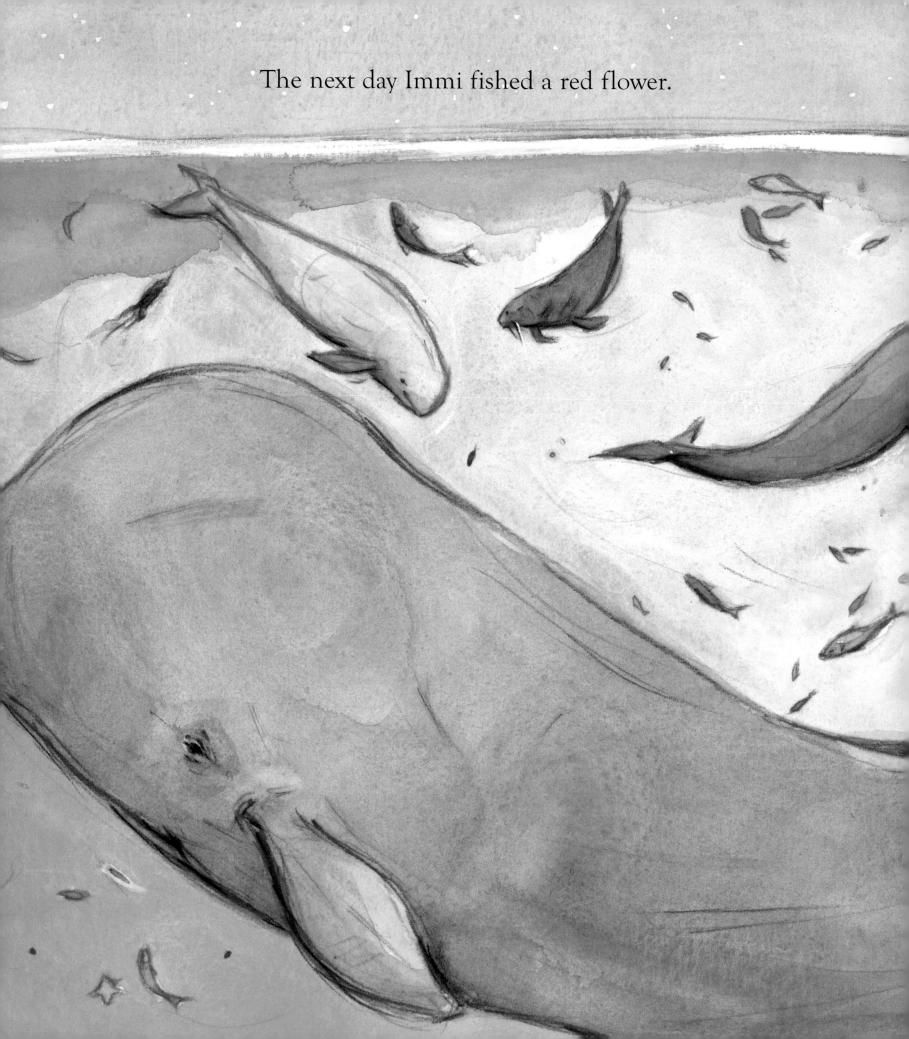

The next day Immi fished a red flower.

Then an
orange starfish . . .

a green leaf . . .

a purple feather . . .

and soon her igloo was the
brightest thing in the land!

It could be seen for miles around.
And, before long, visitors came
from far and wide to
look and to wonder.

They always stayed for supper,
and they filled those long, dark nights
with stories of faraway lands.

And Immi's world seemed a brighter
and more colourful place.

Then one day the ice began to melt.
It was time for her to leave.

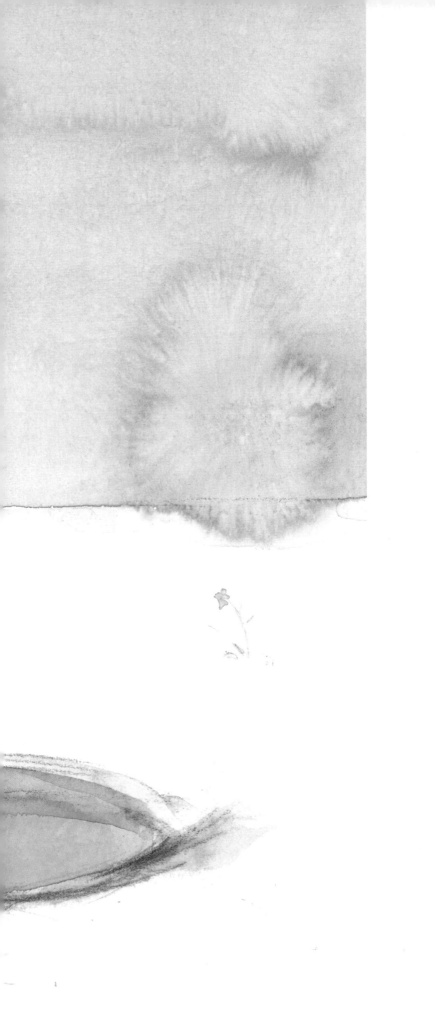

But just as Immi was about to go,
she stopped and put her hand
to her necklace. She took the
small bear and gently
dropped it into the water.

Then she turned and left.

Faraway, a little boy walks across a beach,
holding the brightest thing he can find.
He throws it into the waves and wonders,
as he always does, where it will go.

But this time something catches
his eye, shining in the sand.

It is a beautiful small white bear.
He picks it up and holds it.

Then he hangs it around his neck,
where a little wooden bird
had once hung.

Other books from Karin Littlewood

Moonshadow

written by Gillian Lobel

Led by Grandfather, the swans fly south over sleepy cities and shimmering seas. But suddenly tragedy strikes, and Moonshadow's future is destined to change for ever. . .

'Outstanding storytelling'
SCHOOL LIBRARY JOURNAL

'Enchanting illustrations fill each page'
CHILDREN'S LITERATURE

* * *

The Most Important Gift of All

written by David Conway

What gift should Ama give her new baby brother to welcome him into the world? Offer him love, Grandma Sisi tells her. But where can Ama find this precious gift?

'Achieves the timelessness of an ethnic myth'
BOOKTRUST

'Littlewood's pictures soar . . .
both intimate and reassuring'
PUBLISHERS WEEKLY

Nominated for the KATE GREENAWAY MEDAL

'Exquisite . . . an excellent introduction to a discussion of other cultures or the birth of a sibling'
SCHOOL LIBRARY JOURNAL